GRETEL K

My Sister's an
Alien

Illustrated by Leigh Hobbs

RED FOX

MY SISTER'S AN ALIEN
A RED FOX BOOK 0 09 943367 2

Published in Great Britain by Red Fox,
an imprint of Random House Children's Books

PRINTING HISTORY
First published in Australia by Random House Australia Pty Ltd, 1998
Red Fox edition published, 2002

1 3 5 7 9 10 8 6 4 2

Set in 17/21pt Bembo Schoolbook
Red Fox books are published by Random House Children's Books,
61-63 Uxbridge Road, London W5 5SA,
a division of The Random House Group Ltd,
in Australia by Random House Australia (Pty) Ltd,
20 Alfred Street, Milsons Point, Sydney, NSW 2061, Australia,
in New Zealand by Random House New Zealand Ltd,
18 Poland Road, Glenfield, Auckland 10, New Zealand,
and in South Africa by Random House (Pty) Ltd,
Endulini, 5A Jubilee Road, Parktown 2193, South Africa

THE RANDOM HOUSE GROUP Limited Reg. No. 954009

A CIP catalogue record for this book is available from the British Library.

Printed and bound in Great Britain by Bookmarque Ltd, Croydon, Surrey

A message from your author...

WARNING: DO NOT BE AFRAID, LAUGH RUDELY OR BURP WITH SURPRISE.

In Australia we speak English just like you do but occasionally we use completely different words. For example, we don't say **trousers**, we say **pants**; we don't say **crisps**, we say **chips**; and we don't say **person from England**, we say **Pommie**.

Some of our Aussie words have been changed in this book so that you **Pommies** can understand them, but some of them haven't. So just in case you're wondering what on earth those words mean, let me tell you that **possums** look like fat cats with long bushy tails and they live in trees, **slaters** are primitive insects the size of your fingernail with lots and lots of legs, the **bush telegraph** is just one person telling the next person the latest gossip, and **goannas** are great big lizards that live in the bush (but never ever spread gossip).

**Also available by
Gretel Killeen in Red Fox**

My Sister's a Yo-yo

It's not every day that your sister shrinks to the size of a strawberry, gets tangled in your yo-yo and ends up in outer space . . . but that's what had happened so far today.

Early this morning Zeke got bored while he was sitting in the car waiting for his mum to take him to school, so he burped the alphabet, picked his nose, did a little fart, checked under the seats for jewelled boxes of hidden treasure and found his precious yo-yo instead. Then he offered his sister ten million dollars if she would get out of the car and play yo-yos with him but while she was leaning out of the car she fell out the window, landed in a pothole, got run over by a truck that was carrying a house and got squished to the size of a strawberry. Now, Zeke knew that he had to stretch his sister back to her normal size but before he did that he thought he might whirl his yo-yo on Eppie's head just for a bit of fun, but it got tangled up really badly in her hair and that's when their mum finally came out of the house to drive Eppie and

Zeke to school. So Zeke hid Eppie in the bottom of his school bag and then Eppie ended up getting dropped down a toilet, stuffed in a bin, stuck up a tree, confiscated by the teacher, stolen by a bird, pinched by a puppy, stuck in a bike wheel, grabbed by a garbage truck, mistaken for a tennis ball, stolen by a bully and saved by Zeke who, at the very end of the day, was going to untangle Eppie from the yo-yo and stretch her back to normal size (just in time for Mum to pick them both up from school and never be any the wiser), **but** he unfortunately decided to do some tricks with Eppie attached to the yo-yo first . . . Walk the Dog, Rock the Cradle, Bite Your Bum and Round the World. And it was while he was doing this particular trick that the yo-yo string broke, and off Eppie went . . .

all the way round the world.

So, Eppie was attached to Zeke's yo-yo looping round the planet.

Meanwhile Mum had arrived to collect both her children from school, and Zeke was standing all alone in the playground desperately wondering if he should:

a) tell his mum that her daughter was lost in outer space and somehow, quite skilfully, make it all Eppie's fault

or b) invite all his friends over to help him celebrate the fact that his sister had flown off the face off the Earth and his wish had finally come true.

or c) run after Eppie and try to save
her

or d) just stand there and act like
nothing had happened.

Well, Zeke was feeling a little lazy
and so he chose d) just stand there and
act like nothing had happened. 'Dum
de dum,' he sang to himself. 'Dum de
dum hoola de dum.'

Mum was getting closer so Zeke tried to think of what he might say should his mum happen to ask, 'Do you know where Eppie is?' 'Um, who?' he could say. 'I don't know anyone by that name. Perhaps you mean that poodle over there.' Or else he could say, 'She's gone to play at a friend's? Uh, she's on detention? A wizard put a spell on her and turned her into dog poop.' Or, 'Actually she's been kidnapped, and the kidnappers want a huge ransom that I know we can't afford so I suggest it would be cheaper to buy another sister.'

(Actually, Zeke realised, that last excuse was not a very good one because there's no way anyone would believe that a kidnapper would want a ransom for Eppie. More likely after five minutes with Eppie, the kidnappers would pay Mum to take her back.)

Mum was waving. She was getting

close. 'Act normal,' thought Zeke, 'act normal.'

She was coming closer and he was nearly acting normal except that he was bouncing up and down like a tennis ball and opening and closing his mouth so fast he looked like a mixture of a wide-mouthed frog and windscreen wipers stuck on **FAST**. (Please note that although boys do often act very weird this is not what Zeke normally looks like.)

'Oh my goodness,' thought Zeke. 'I should quit bouncing, shut my mouth and stop my eyes from blinking because otherwise Mum will definitely get suspicious and even though she won't know exactly what's happened she'll punish me anyway. It could be terrible, it could be horrible: much worse than having a sister!'

But actually Zeke need not have

worried, because his mum didn't seem to notice anything odd at all and walked straight past him to the middle of the playground where she bent down and kissed a small tree.

'Yahoooooooooooooooooo,' Zeke whispered softly. 'Mum's forgotten her glasses again.'

'Perfect,' thought Zeke. 'Mum's blind as a bat and there's no way I'm telling her where her glasses are.' (You see, much as Zeke adored his mum, he rather enjoyed his life as well, and although he apparently talked far too much in class and only tried half as hard as he could, Zeke was smart enough to realise that if he told his mum where her glasses were she would immediately see that Eppie was missing and he would of course cop all the blame.) So Zeke said nothing and ran off to the school sports equipment room where he borrowed a tennis racquet.

'Hi, Mum,' said Zeke when he returned and gave his mum a peck on the cheek.

'Hello, darling. Have you seen Eppie?'

'Yes, she's here,' said Zeke holding up the tennis racquet. 'But she's lost her voice so she can't say too much.'

'Oh dear,' said Mum. 'Eppie's voice probably just needs a rest. Voices get tired too, you know.' And with that Mum kissed the tennis racquet on the head, said 'there, there' and the three of them got into the car.

During the drive home Mum sang her favourite song, *Achy Breaky Heart*, which made all the dogs they passed on the way howl very loudly. Zeke was of course completely embarrassed, but when you're in the middle of pretending your sister is a tennis racquet you are really in no position at all to criticise others.

And so, instead of groaning and rolling his eyes as he normally would when his mum sang *Achy Breaky Heart*, Zeke decided to pick a fight with the tennis racquet, just so Mum would think everything was normal.

'M-u-m, Eppie's pinching me,' said Zeke. 'Mu-u-um, she's kicking me. Mu-u-um, Eppie just poked her tongue out!'

'Quiet, you two,' said Mum as she drove with her head stuck right out the window because she thought it might help her see a little better.

'Quiet, you two, or you'll have no TV for the rest of your lives.'

'Good,' said Zeke to himself. 'Mum doesn't suspect a thing.'

Once they got home, things were really pretty good for a while. Zeke of course got to eat twice as much afternoon tea and when Mum realised that Eppie hadn't eaten a crumb she sent the tennis racquet off to bed.

'I'll take her,' said Zeke, acting really kind. 'You just keep looking for your glasses.'

'Oh that's so sweet of you,' said Mum. 'And when you get back down we'll have a nice piece of chocolate cake.'

('Actually,' Zeke thought, 'I'd rather have a new yo-yo.')

All alone in Eppie's room, he tucked the tennis racquet into bed, looked around and quietly began to think seriously what the rest of his life would be like without his little sister . . . 'Fantastic!' he decided.

That night Zeke got to watch whatever he wanted on TV, his mother did nearly all his homework, and he got to stay up extra late. But then, just when he was about to clean his teeth and go to bed, his mum said, 'I'll be up in a minute to give you a hug. I'll just give Eppie her cuddle first.'

'No!' yelled Zeke, jumping up from the couch. 'You can't hug her . . . because . . . because . . . because . . . because for all we know she might have some disgusting disease where your ears blow up . . . and your nose explodes . . . and your legs and arms fall off. You can't hug her. If you do, you might die! And then I'd die of starvation and Gran and Pops would die of shock and then all the neighbours would come to look at our bodies and they'd catch the disease and they'd all die and all their friends and relatives too. So basically, Mum, if you go up and hug Eppie now you could end up killing at the very least forty-seven thousand million people and their pets who need to be fed!'

'Zeke, sick little children need to hug their mothers, so I simply must hug Eppie. But if it will make you worry any less, I'll tie a hanky round my mouth and stick a peg on my nose. Now then, I'll look for my glasses for just one more minute and then I'll be up to hug you both.'

'Oh no,' thought Zeke. 'What should I do? My life is about to be completely over and I never even got to grow my hair really long and play the drums in a rock band. If Mum finds her glasses and sees that Eppie's a tennis racquet I am definitely going to be dead. Oh, please somebody save me!!!!!!!!!!!!'

Now sometimes, if you make enough wishes throughout your life and none of them ever comes true, the wish accountants who wear suits and live up in the clouds realise that you're owed a really big wish, and that's the wish they'll try to fulfil. Get it? So that's what happened to Zeke. He hadn't had any wishes come true for ages and ages (except the wish that his sister would disappear, but that one didn't really count because she was still haunting him anyway). So the wish accountants decided it was time for Zeke to be given a really, really big wish and they made this wish come true. (Of course this meant that none of his other wishes would ever come true: he would never win the lottery or be given a Ferrari or represent Australia playing football . . . but Zeke decided he'd just happily blame Eppie for all of this.)

So what do you think happened? Do you think Zeke's strawberry-sized sister suddenly dropped from the skies and came plonking down the chimney, where she got stuck just long enough in the grate for Zeke to pull her out by her feet and stretch her back to normal size, so their mother never discovered there'd been one single problem and they lived happily ever after and became incredibly rich and all became actors on *Neighbours*?

Brrrrrrrrrrrrrrr, drum roll please!

No, nothing so fabulously exciting unfortunately. What happened exactly then and there was that the family cat walked past Zeke, and he was wearing Zeke's mother's glasses. Fantastic! Mum wouldn't find them for a million years.

The cat often secretly borrowed glasses because he liked to read, but his eyesight was getting worse. Of course he knew that he really should go to the

eye doctor and get his own set of reading glasses, but the nearest animal eye doctor was a dog and there was no way this cat was going there.

'Thanks, wish accountants,' Zeke said to the ceiling. 'Although I do agree with the kids who are reading this book and think you really could have done a whole lot better and just dropped Eppie down the chimney.' Then Zeke grabbed the biggest fattest book he could find (a cookbook on one thousand and one things to do with fish), showed it to the cat and put the book and the cat outside the back door. 'Enjoy your read,' he said to the cat. 'And take all the time you want.'

Then Zeke went back inside.
'This is great,' thought Zeke. 'Mum

won't find her glasses for ages now.' And he sat down to relax, put his feet up on the coffee table, stick his finger in his ear and see if any mice were living in there. But suddenly he interrupted himself as he shrieked, 'Oh no,' and got such a shock he jabbed his finger so far into his ear that it almost popped out the other side. 'I forgot that in about twenty seconds Mum's going upstairs to kiss a tennis racquet goodnight!' said Zeke. 'I'd better go and find an ugly doll that Mum can cuddle instead.'

But up in Eppie's bedroom there was no doll that looked at all like Eppie (who by the way is not ugly and does not look like half a worm, no matter what Zeke says). There were seven Barbie dolls and a stuffed monkey and although Zeke thought the stuffed monkey did look a bit like his sister it was way too small.

Stomp, bump, crash, ow! It was his mother coming up the stairs. And so in absolute desperation, Zeke opened Eppie's wardrobe door, rummaged through her clothes, found a nightie, put it on, stuck a ribbon in his hair, jumped straight into his little sister's bed and pretended to be asleep . . . just in the nick of time.

'How are you feeling, Eppie?' said Mum to the bedside lamp. 'Still can't talk? Well never mind. Let Mummy give you a hug to make you a whole lot better.' First Mum hugged the bedside lamp, then the chest of drawers, the little chair, the beanbag, the desk and the footstool until finally she'd gone all the way round the room, tripped on the carpet, fallen onto the bed, and given Zekeppie her hug.

'Eeeeeeeek!' squeaked Zeke, trying to sound like a girl.

'In the morning, as a special treat, we'll do your hair in braids,' said Mum. 'And if you're too sick to go off to school you can play with some of my make-up. In fact,' she paused for extra excitement, 'would you like to put on a little lipstick now, just to make you feel pretty?'

'Help,' thought Zeke. 'I'd rather fall

into a black hole and spend the rest of my life being cuddled by slaters than wear one crumb of make-up.'

'Here's a beautiful red lipstick,' said his mother. 'So you can sleep looking just like Snow White.' And she put the lipstick on Zeke, tucked him into bed, kissed him goodnight, said, 'Sleep tight, Eppie. I'll just walk down the hall now and say sweet dreams to Zeke.'

Zeke waited calmly until his mother left the room and then he went into a complete panic. He waved his arms and his legs like an upside down cockroach, covered his face with Eppie's pillow and screamed like Tarzan . . .

aaaaa aaaa aaaaaaaaaaaa a aaaa aaaa aaaa aa

And then when he'd finished he caught a look at the pillow that was covering his face, saw a red lipsticked mouth smudged on it and screamed once more, only more softly, aaaaaaaaaaaaagh. Gross.

'What will I do?' agonised Zeke. 'I'll never get back into my room in time for Mum to kiss me goodnight!' He wriggled and squirmed in desperate panic, fell off the bed and rolled around, more and more and more until suddenly he found himself wrapped tight in the lambswool rug that normally lay on Eppie's floor. And that's when he caught another glimpse of himself in Eppie's bedroom mirror. 'I look almost exactly like a sheep,' he thought. 'Especially to someone who isn't wearing her glasses.' And with that he got on all fours while still wrapped in the rug and went charging down the hall to his bedroom, bleating 'Baaaaaaa' as he passed his mum.

Once in his room Zeke unwrapped himself, shoved the rug into his cupboard and dived into his bed.

'Good heavens, darling,' his mother said to his baseball mit as she bumbled through the door, 'I really must be very tired, because I've started seeing things.'

And with that the cat came barging through the door wearing Mum's glasses and carrying Mum's biggest fattest cookbook (about one thousand and one things to do with fish). Well of course Mum fainted onto the bed and fell flat on top of Zeke.

'Oh,' mumbled Zeke. 'I should have remembered that stupid cat did a speed reading course.'

So there Zeke was, still wearing his sister's nightie and a pretty pink bow in his hair, pinned underneath his collapsed mother. She was still as still and not saying a word and Zeke was

worried that she might really have
injured herself . . . until he heard her
start to snore and mumble, 'Oh yes,
Leonardo di Caprio! Come and rescue
me!'

   But what was Eppie doing all this
time? Had she stopped flying round
the world and landed in some
extraordinary place? Was she skiing
Swiss slopes, fishing in Finland, surfing
in Samoa, digging diamonds in Dubai
or swimming in the sea with silly seals?

Or was she still as small as a strawberry, attached to Zeke's yo-yo and flying round the world, getting giddier and giddier and giddier and yelling, 'Pass me a bucket! I think I'm going to be sick.'

Well, I'll tell you. She did fly round and round and round the world high up in the sky, but then after a while she started to drift down, closer and closer to earth. France was right there underneath her and she was just about to get spiked in the bottom by the Eiffel Tower when she flapped her arms like a bird to raise herself higher and was caught by a giant gust of hot air that pushed her up safe above the poking point. And the gust of wind blew her on and on.

'I could fly all the way home like this,' thought Eppie as she flap flap flapped away.

As she flew over America a group of

farmers tried to shoot her, a flock of
lazy finches perched on her shoulders as
they migrated to Brazil, the Tahitians
tried to catch her in a net and put her
in the zoo, and in England they wanted
to eat her. But strawberry-sized Eppie
flapped on and on until finally she got
so exhausted that she caught the nearest

passing cloud, sat on it and had a little snooze.

The sun was warm and snug as it shone down on the cloud but as Eppie slept, more and more clouds joined onto hers. Clouds joined to the sides, below and above until the whole sky was filled with clouds, the sun was hidden and Eppie got cold. And that's when she woke up.

'Hey, how come it's so dark?' Eppie wondered. 'It couldn't be night time yet.' A crack of thunder and a blaze of lightning and a most frightening roar of wind followed – rushing, howling, bellowing louder. And before Eppie could click her heels and say, 'There's No Place Like Home,' she was caught inside the most terrifying twister.

Round and round and round she spun, higher, faster, all in a twirl. 'I'm going to die,' Eppie gasped. 'I'm going to be sucked up, twisted and spat out. I'll never be able to see Mum again. I'll never eat ice cream or see my school friends or play at the beach or have another birthday. Oh this is an absolute disaster – except for one amazing thing: Zeke is going to get blamed for it!'

And with that Eppie was squeezed up higher into the tornado and whirled like a banana in a blender (and let me say here that it was just as well that she had tied her shoelaces with a double bow because otherwise there is no way her shoes would have stayed on).

Now one of the good things about
being twisted and turned and spun
around if you are a girl who has been
squashed to the size of a strawberry is
that all of the tugging and pulling and
whirling around does tend to stretch
you back to normal size. So that's what
happened to Eppie. Then there was a
great big pop, like the sound you make
with your finger and your mouth but
much, much louder.

pop

and Eppie was blurted right out of that twister and upupup into space where she floated around for quite a while and then landed

thump

on a place called Planet Sock.

Meanwhile Zeke was still lying on his bed wearing his sister's nightie, a pink bow in his hair and a smudge of his mother's bright red lipstick, and being squished under the heavy sleeping weight of his absolutely exhausted mother, who you may remember had just begun to snore. The room shook with every rumbling snort, the curtains flapped, the bed springs groaned and a gust of humphy-galumphy Mum-snore-air would go right up Zeke's nose and nearly make his hair blow off.

This torture continued for quite some time until Zeke got completely and utterly fed up and yelled out, 'Oh, bottom!' (because he wasn't allowed to say 'bum'). 'This is terrible,' he said. 'With all this noise the police are definitely going to come here to see what all the fuss is and try to rescue our family, but they'll only find Mum and me and they'll guess Eppie's been killed by Mum's elephant snoring – maybe sucked up her nose and got stuck in her brain. And then they'll have to take Mum's head off and clean her brain with a vacuum cleaner to look for Eppie and they won't find her of course and all the police and doctors will be so upset that they'll stop concentrating and probably sew Mum's head back on round the wrong way, which will make it impossible for her to sit down and have dinner with us, let alone hug us goodnight. Oh bottom, bottom, bottom.'

'Stop snoring, Mum!' Zeke ordered urgently. But it was too late, because just then there was a tap tap tap on the window and he looked up in fright. But it wasn't the police; it was, to Zeke's surprise, the three possums who lived in the attic. They were dressed in their party gear, bright frocks and floral shirts, and were very very mad.

'What on earth do you think you're doing down here?' asked the biggest possum whose name was Ralph Gorgeous. 'We're trying to have a party upstairs and no one can even hear the band because of this terrible, deafening, rumbling noise. It's making the whole house shake and shake and making our fabulous party drinks spill all over our lovely fur coats.'

'I'm sorry,' said Zeke. 'The noise is my mother. She's really tired from looking for her glasses, which are actually being worn by the cat. But I couldn't tell her that because if Mum had her glasses, then she would have seen that my stinker sister is nowhere to be found. So Mum would have asked me, "Zeke, where on earth is Eppie?" And I would have had to say, "Well actually, Mum, she's not on Earth at all; she's attached to my yo-yo and is flying round the world . . . oh and by the way she's shrunk to the size of a strawberry."

'And then of course Mum would have got absolutely furious and confiscated the rest of my life . . . and that's probably exactly what she will do when she wakes up . . . straight after she's killed me!'

Then Zeke burst into tears (but he pretended that he just had a cold), gave a great big blow on his nose and then wiped the snot all over his sleeve.

'Ar yuk!' said the second possum whose name was Fluffybigbum. 'Don't be such an animal!'

'Do you think you could help me?' Zeke asked the three possums as they sat perched on the window dressed in their party clothes which didn't really fit because they'd been pinched from neighbours' clotheslines. 'Could you spread the word on the bush telegraph? Perhaps ask the flying fish, or the secretive snakes or those gossiping goannas . . . just spread the word that we need to find where Eppie is because, much to my regret, we have to get her back.'

'Don't be ridiculous,' said the third possum, whose name was Nosewhistle Jo. 'Asking animals one by one – I've never heard of anything so primitive.'

'You're right, of course,' Zeke replied. 'I should hire a plane that writes in the sky,

lost:
one stupid strawberry-sized sister, contact
Zeke,
and don't tell my mum.'

'Are you joking?' said Ralph Gorgeous. 'Or has some horrible slug slid in your ear and into your head and eaten half your brain? Because if you really want to find where Eppie is quick smart, I suggest you hop on the Internet.'

'But I don't know how to use the Internet,' moaned Zeke.

'Then we'll find Wise Old Owl and he can teach you,' said Nosewhistle Jo as he whistled *Hey diddly* through his nose.

'Well could you help get me out from under here first?' said Zeke in a muffled voice as his mother made one more enormous snore, rolled smack bang on top of him and said, 'I love you too, Tom Cruise.'

'Quick! Get me out of here!' said Zeke, and with that Fluffybigbum jumped off the windowsill and into the bedroom, walked straight up to Mum and said in a very deep voice, 'Hello, I'm Tom Cruise. Follow me.' And up Mum got and followed Fluffybigbum the possum all the way down the hall and safely to Mum's room, where she fell fast asleep once more, snoring like a dillion pigs.

Then, before you could make whatever sound it is that a wise old bird could make, bwa bwa, bwa perhaps, the Wise Old Owl flew in through the window

with a flurry of feathers and smashed
straight into the mirror. 'Ow!' said Owl.
'Those mirrors are horrid. Every time I
look in one I think I've seen the most
beautiful bird and break my beak
trying to kiss it.'

'Are you sure this is the *Wise* Old Owl?' whispered Zeke to Nosewhistle Jo.

But it *was* the Wise Old Owl and pretty soon he was setting up the computer to send Zeke's message and find out just who in the world knew where Eppie was. 'This plug here, that button there, put this thingummyjig in that what-not,' said the Wise Old Owl as he ordered everybody in the room to assist with his important task. 'OK,' he said finally. 'Now we're ready to type the message.'

'Message typed,' replied Zeke with pride.

'And now we shall send it off round the world,' bellowed the Wise Old Owl triumphantly. 'Watch me press this little red power switch.' And the whole thing went . . .

Kaboom.

In fact the message wasn't sent to computers all round the world, but printed instead on each of the Wise Old Owl's feathers, which had blown right off in the explosion and were now fluttering high into the sky to be spread by the world's wandering winds.

'Oh no, I'm naked!' said the Wise Old
Owl. 'But at least the message has been
sent. Could someone hand me a
dressing gown while we wait for our
replies?'

Well Ralph Gorgeous lent Owl his
leopard skin coat and then they waited.

Wait, wait, wait, wait.

'Want a chocolate biscuit?' Zeke asked the Wise Old Owl.

'No thanks. I'm on a diet,' he replied.

Wait, wait, wait, wait.

And then with a hum and a whirr and a whiz, messages started flying in from every single corner of the globe . . . and some even came with photos. Yes, photos of what looked like a strawberry with something attached to its head. 'I wonder how they took those photos of Eppie?' thought Zeke. 'Cameras always break when I try to photograph her.'

Someone even sent in a video in which you could very clearly see that Eppie was singing that song that made Zeke want to vomit every time he heard it, *I'm a Barbie Girl in a Barbie World!*

She'd been seen over Botswana, Croatia, Canada, Tasmania and

Scandinavia. Some cow even sent a message to say she'd seen Eppie jumping over the moon.

But the most recent sighting had been by two astrologers who were visiting their mummies in Egypt.

They said they'd seen a girl dancing way out on Planet Sock who was singing a little song to herself called *My Brother Zeke is a Boy's Bra.*

'That's her. That's her!' yelled happy Zeke. 'That's my horrible, disgusting, worm head, pig's bottom, bosom brain sister. Yahoo! Let's go get her!'

'Not us,' said Ralph Gorgeous. 'We've got a party to go to and, besides, we've done all we can.'

'Well if there's anything I can ever do for you,' said Zeke, 'just plop down through that manhole in the ceiling.'

'Possumhole,' corrected Nosewhistle Jo.

'Actually, Zeke,' said Fluffybigbum,

'could I borrow that pretty dress you're wearing?'

Zeke had forgotten he was wearing Eppie's nightie and was so embarrassed he shrieked, 'Aeiou!' ran from the room and tumble, tumble, tumbled down the stairs like a tennis ball.

And that's where he lay like a spilt laundry basket and dreamt that he blew up a thousand balloons, tied all of their strings to his belt and floated up, right up into space where he found his sister Eppie and made her promise that she would pay him a fee of a thousand dollars a week for the rest of their lives for the privilege of being his sister.

But then Zeke woke up and unfortunately remembered all the trouble that he was in.

'Oh no, oh no, a few hours to go before Mum wakes up and Eppie and my yo-yo are still lost in space. How am I ever going to get up there?' he wondered as he lay on the floor rattling away, listening to his mother snore. 'You can't get a bus to space, or catch a train, or a plane, or walk, or run, or roll or skateboard or . . . Hey, wait, I know! I could go to a circus, dress up as a clown and get them to blow me out of the cannon . . . off the face of earth and into the starry skies . . . or if that didn't work and the worst came to the worst I could fall in a pothole, get run over by a truck that is towing a house, get shrunk to the size of a strawberry, attached to a yo-yo and hurled into the sky like a rocket . . . Hey wait a minute!' said Zeke to himself. 'That's it – a rocket!'

Well of course Zeke tried to make his own space rocket using old toilet rolls, egg cartons and silver foil but the glue wouldn't dry and there was no sister to sit on things to make them stick better (because she was selfishly dancing on Planet Sock) and no mum to help with the cutting out (because she was upstairs, begging Tom Cruise to marry her, in between snoring like a fart cushion) and so in the end he snuck out

the door, got on his bike and rode to
the nearest space centre.

'Hello,' Zeke said, when the space
centre's door was opened by a huge
toothless purple-haired woman. 'Excuse
me for bothering you so late in the
night but I'd like to go on your next
trip into space.'

'Oh, that's nice,' said the toothless
purple-haired woman. 'But I'm very
sorry you can't come because what we
need is males who are strong, brave and

SPACE CENTRE

fearless; we have enough little girls with
bows in their hair.'

'**What!**' gasped Zeke. Oh yes, the
nightie, and off he rode home to
quickly change into his Superboy suit

and once again knock on the space centre door.

'I'm very sorry, Superboy,' said the toothless purple-haired woman, 'but I'm afraid you're far too young.'

And with that Zeke said thank you and rode off into the night. Only to return ten minutes later wearing a false beard and a moustache.

'I'm very sorry, Mister Super,' said the toothless purple-haired woman, 'you're absolutely perfect except for one simple thing: you are far too thin.'

And off rode Zeke as fast as he could to find cotton wool to stick in his cheeks, and pillows to stuff down his suit so that every single part of his body seemed quite enormous and he looked like a balloon filled with marbles . . . and he could hardly move.

S l o w l y Zeke got back onto his bike and s l o w l y he reached for the pedals and ever so s l o w l y he began to ride back to the space centre.

'I'm terribly sorry,' said the toothless purple-haired woman. 'I'm sure you'd make the perfect astronaut, but you're just a moment too late. If you'd been here even a minute ago things might have been quite different but, as it happens, today's space probe is now full and leaving any second.'

'Bup!' said Zeke with his cheeks full of cotton wool. 'Bup, bup, bup, bup!' But the toothless purple-haired woman had already left, to eat mashed peanut butter and melted ice cream (mixed with a pinch of salt and scrambled snails) while she watched the latest space rocket take-off.

So Zeke stumbled along in his fat

Superboy suit, beard and moustache, desperately looking for a way to get past the locked wire fences and onto the launch pad.

'Who's there?' said a voice from out on the tarmac.

'Pleath blet me in plast thith gade,' repeated Zeke.

'Listen, old fellow,' said the voice. 'Swallow whatever you've got in your mouth, then come here and tell me what you said.'

And so Zeke removed all the pillows and stuffing and his beard and moustache. Then he slipped under the big wire fence to walk towards the voice. And when he got right up to the voice, he found himself talking to the space rocket flight attendant who was dressed in a very nice, casual outfit with matching tie and little peaked cap. The attendant was just about to fasten all doors and check that all seatbelts were fastened when Zeke said, 'Wait! I need a lift into space.'

'Sorry, Superboy,' said the attendant. 'We just gave the last seat to a shooting star who's a little bit sick with the flu. So you'll have to catch the next probe which leaves in about . . . oh,' and with that the attendant looked at his watch. 'In about eleven years. Now get off the launching pad if you don't mind and go and stand somewhere safe.'

10 9 8 7

Are you thinking, Poor Zeke, he's missed his chance?

6 5 4

Well, not on your life!

3 2 1

Because what do you see if you look very closely?

ZEROBLASTOFF!

Look, right there on the pointy bit. Do you see a little person dressed as Superboy sort of making a face like he's sitting on something sharp? Well, guess who that is? It's Zeke, blasting through space with his mouth so wide open that he's just swallowed three flies and a pigeon.

Up, up, up he went, through the clouds,

through the blue skies and beyond. Up
to the rainbow, through the red, orange,
yellow, green, blue, indigo, violet, and up
into space, dark space where a zillion
stars were twinkling brightly saying,
'Zekie, come and play with me.'

After seven hours, or maybe five
minutes, Zeke's bottom really began to
hurt. So he tried to get more
comfortable by doing a shift and a

wiggle but he slipped completely off
the tip and began to slide down the
space probe. 'Uh oh,' said Zeke.

He tried to wrap his arms round the
space probe, but he just kept slip sliding
down. Down he slipped, down, down,
his eyes wide open with fear. He tried
to grab hold of a wing as he slid, he
tried to grab on with his legs. But
down he slid with the engine flames
getting closer. He was hot and scared
and his hands were all slippery and he
was gaining speed . . . when all of a
sudden he came to a halt as his
Superboy suit got caught on the corner
of the window and Zeke took a peek
inside.

'Hello!' he called to the silver-suited
astronauts as he tap tapped on the
glass. 'Hello!' he bellowed. 'Could you
help me, please?' But nobody heard
him because they were all eating

spacecorn, which is like popcorn only a gillion times louder. That's right, nobody paid him any attention at all until all of a sudden the space probe took a sharp turn to the left and Zeke was hurled at the window and his face squished up hard on the glass. The astronauts heard a tremendous thump, looked up to see Zeke's flat face, and then all fainted into their spacecorn buckets.

'Oh fabulous,' said Zeke, dangling from the window. 'Help me, you great fat burp heads!' And then he quietly began to cry, feeling very sorry for himself until he was rudely interrupted by a gentle rrrrrrrrrrripping sound. 'My suit!' shrieked Zeke. 'My Superboy suit is tearing!' And sure enough it was.

'This is all Eppie's fault,' mumbled Zeke bitterly. as finally his suit tore completely off and once again he was caught in his undies. (Yep! The Barbie ones his mum gave him for Christmas last year, nineteen pairs for the price of one.) 'Help!' he screamed into the dark universe, as he was hurtled through the atmosphere.

'Help, help,' he called as he raced through the galaxy at a billion trillion zillion dillion hillion kilometres an hour. 'Heeeeeeeeeeeeeeeeeeeeeeeeeeeeeeeeeee eeeeeeeeeeeeeeeeeeeeeeeeeeeeeeeeeeeeee

eeeeeeeeeeeeeeeeeeeeeeeeeeeeeeeeeeeeeee
eeeeeeeeeeeeeeeeeeeeeeeeeeeeeeeeeeeeeeee
eeeeeeeeeeeeeeeeeeeeeeeeeeeeeeeeeeeeeeee
eeeeeeeeeeeeeeeeeeeeeeeeeeeeeeeeeeeeeeee
eeeeeeeeeeeeeeeeeeeeeeeeeeeeeeeeeeeeeeee
eeeeeeeeeeeeeeeeeeeeeeeeeeeeeeeeeeeeeeee
eeeeeeeeeeeeeeeeeeeeeeeeeeeeeeeeeeeeeeee
eeeeeeeeeeeeeeeeeeeeeeeeeeeeeeeeeeeeeeee
eeeeeeeeeeeeeeeeeeeeeeeeeeeeeeeeeeeeeeee
eeeeeeeeeeeeeeeeeeeeeeeeeeeeeeeeeeeeeeee
eeeeeeeeeeeeeeeeeeeeeeeeeeeeeeeeeeeeeeee

eeeeeeeeeeeeeeeeeeeeeeeeeeeeeeeeeeeeeeee
eeeeeeeeeeeeeeeeeeeeeeeeeeeeeeeeeeeeeeee
eeeeeeeeeeeeeeeeeeeeeeeeeeeeeeeeeeeeeeee
eeeeeeeeeeeeeeeeeeeeeeeeeeeeeeeeeeeeeeee
eeeeeeeeeeeeeeeeeeeeeeeeeeeeeeeeeeeeeeee
eeeeeeeeeeeeeeeeeeeeeeeeeeeeeeeeeeeeeeee
eeeeeeeeeeeeeeeeeeeeeeeeeeeeeeeeeeeeeeee
eeeeeeeeeeeeeeeeeeeeeeeeeeeeeeeeeeeeeeee
eeeeeeeeeeeeeeeeeeeeeeeeeeeeeeeeeeeeeeee
eeeeeeeeeeeeeeeeeeeeeeeeeeeeeeeeeeeeeeee
eeeeeeeeeeeeeeeeeeeeeeeeeeeeeeeeeeeeeeee
eeeeeeeeeeeeeeeeeeeeeeeeeeeeeeeeeeeeeeee
eeeeeeeeeeeeeeeeeeeeeeeeeeeeeeeeeeeeeeee
eeeeeeeeeeeeeeeeeeeeeeeeeeeeeeeeeeeeeeee
eeeeeeeeeeeeeeeeeeeeeeeeeeeeeeeeeeeeeeee
eeeeeeeeeeeeeeeeeeelp!'

'Don't cry, my little fellow,' said the
kind deep voice of the Man in the
Moon as he caught Zeke in his great
big hand. 'Here, put this cheese suit on
and cover up those Barbie Doll undies.'

'I can't wear a suit made out of cheese,' replied Zeke.

'Oh, all right then,' said the Man in the Moon. 'If you want everyone to see your . . .'

'OK, OK,' interrupted Zeke as he grabbed the suit made of cheese, while the Man in the Moon whispered in his ear, 'My mum gave me twelve pairs of Barbie Doll undies for my birthday, and boy do I know they're embarrassing.'

Once he was dressed in the cheese suit, which I must say wasn't all that warm because it was full of holes, Zeke told the Man in the Moon all about strawberry-sized Eppie, the possums, the owl, the Internet, the kaboom, the astronomers, and even his mother's loud snoring.

'So that's what that dreadful noise is,' said the Man in the Moon.

And sure enough, when Zeke stopped
sobbing, even though he was sitting on
the moon, he could still hear his
mother's dreadful snorts.

'So you see, my sister Eppie was last seen up in space and I absolutely have to find her before my mum wakes up and blames me and yells and screams and carries on until my ears burst and my head explodes and I'm stuffed and put in a museum. And besides,' Zeke continued very softly, 'I want my yo-yo back.'

'Oh I understand,' said the Man in the Moon, or Moonie as he liked to be called. 'I used to have a yo-yo myself but I dropped it one day and it fell to Earth . . . and created the Grand Canyon I believe. But enough of that. Tell me, son, where was little Eppie last seen?'

'Well some astronomers saw her on Planet Sock. Do you know where that is?'

'Haven't got a clue,' said Moonie. 'But I've got a Planet Directory. Let's hop on my new space motorbike, take it for a spin and find this sister of yours.' And that's exactly what they set off to do.

They jumped onto Moonie's lovely cheese space motorbike and went racing off the surface of the moon, far away and into space, stopping off at the Milky Way to get a couple of milkshakes.

'Yeehaa!' they both squealed and they giggled so hard that they nearly fell off twice.

'Hold on tight,' said the Man in the Moon. 'And keep your eye out for dangerous unidentified flying objects.'

'You mean aliens?' asked Zeke.

'No. I mean humans in silver suits eating spacecorn and fainting while they career around the neighbourhood in space rockets,' said Moonie.

And so they sped through space, ducking and weaving round all the stars, in a sky space called Hollywood, then through bright light and into black holes, all the while laughing and giggling and fighting over who was taking up too much of the seat. And then with a sudden screech of brakes Moonie said, 'First stop, Pluto for petrol.'

On Pluto, they checked the Planet Directory but couldn't find Planet Sock anywhere, so they asked the petrol attendant who was a dribbling big-eared pup.

'Dar,' he said in a deep slow voice. 'Um ah I don't know. Try the next stop. Those Martians know lots of things.'

And so Moonie and Zeke rode to Mars, which is a planet made of chocolate with a caramel centre, and they asked two flubbery Martians if they knew where Planet Sock was, but their ears were so covered with folds of fat that they couldn't even hear the question.

Next stop was Venus, the planet of love, and Zeke and Moonie hadn't even turned off the engine before a hundred long-haired girls ran up and tried to cuddle them. 'Oh puke,' said Zeke and the Man in the Moon. 'Let's get out of here! Girls' germs, girls' germs,' they both screamed together and off they went, scared to billyo that they might be hugged and kissed to death.

So, finally, completely covered in kiss marks and desperate for a scrub-a-dub wash, they landed on Neptune to ask if anybody knew of Planet Sock.

Well now, Planet Neptune is ruled by a giant fish with a long flowing beard and long flowing hair and an enormous fork. He's bad and mean and mighty unclean, afraid of no one except barbers and baths.

'Oh pong!' said Zeke. 'This guy smells worse than Eppie.' And on they went to ask their question.

'Excuse me, sir,' said the Man in the Moon pinching his nose tightly. 'You don't habben to doe where a place called Pladed Sog bight be?'

'Of course I do, but I'm not telling

you,' roared the King. 'Now get out of here!'

'Bud please, sir,' continued brave Zeke while he also pinched his nose tight. 'I deed to doe where Pladed Sog is so I cad fide by sisda.'

'Sister?' bellowed the King. 'She wouldn't happen to be beautiful, would she?'

'Dot in de least,' said Zeke disgustedly.

'Eppie looks like a plasticine chihuahua.'

'Well I've heard on the satellite that a beautiful girl landed on Planet Sock. She arrived wearing some sort of round crown on her head and the people there made her their queen.'

'Oh, my gosh!' gasped Zeke in a whisper. 'That round crown is my precious yo-yo and so the girl wearing it must be Eppie. But how could anyone think that she was beautiful, when she looks like an ugly chihuahua?'

'I heard that,' boomed the mighty mean Neptune. 'And how dare you speak badly of my son's future wife!'

'Wod?' said Zeke. 'You bust be jokig.'

'Do I look like I have a sense of humour?' grumped King Neptune.

'Doe,' said Zeke quietly, 'bud you loog lige you should ged wud.'

'Get out of my sight!' thundered Neptune.

'Doe, waid!' said Moonie. 'We deed to find de girl.'

'Well I'm damned if I'm going to tell you where she is,' laughed the King, 'because we're off to get her for ourselves.'

And with that Neptune and his son Nipper slid onto their beautiful flying white horses and charged off to Planet Sock.

'Follow those horses,' Zeke yelled to Moonie, who was so impressed by the Neptunes' horsepower he was thinking he should possibly get a faster space motorbike.

'Follow them, please!' screeched Zeke one more time.

'Pardon?' said Moonie in a daze.

'Oh forget it,' said Zeke as he grabbed for the space motorbike. 'Just hop onto the back.'

Well now, I don't know if you've ridden a space motorbike made of cheese, but it's not that easy to do. Especially if you've got a huge Man in the Moon plopped heavily on the back. Vroooooooooooooooooooooooooooooooom went the engine, then they both tumbled off.

Then they clambered back on and the engine vroomed again and they kangaroo-hopped along the surface of Planet Neptune until they tipped over once again.

'Oh for heaven's sake, let me do it,' said Moonie.

'No,' said Zeke. 'It's my turn.'

'But it's my bike.'

'Well it's my turn.'

'My bike.'

'My turn.'

And so they continued arguing like seagulls until the flapping wings of the flying horses could no longer be heard.

Then Zeke said, 'Hey, what's that over

there?' and while Moonie turned to look at absolutely nothing, Zeke hopped on the bike and headed off into space with Moonie hanging on the back. But unfortunately, not for long.

'Weeeooo, weeooo,' came the sound of the Planet Police sirens. 'Weeooo, weeooo. Pull over or we'll be forced to shoot!'

So Zeke of course did pull over with a bump and a screech, and the Planet Police pulled up right beside him on their brand new glowing gold spaceboards.

'You're both under arrest for driving dangerously and must come with us to the police station,' said the two little crimson police dressed in their cool sky surfing gear.

Zeke and Moonie wanted to escape but didn't have a sultana-sized idea how. So they hopped on the back of the spaceboards and caught the waves and currents of the heavens towards the station. That is until they were suddenly ambushed by a spaceship full of screaming girls from Venus.

'Hi, boys. We've come to rescue you!' squealed the girlie girls. And that's exactly what they did. They swooped by on their pretty pink skycycles, plonked the boys on the handlebars, and then pedalled far away.

It was great, they had escaped, but there was still a problem because the girls had no desire to chase Neptune and Nipper all the way to Planet Sock. That's right: the girls wanted to go dancing with Zeke and Moonie, then play hide and seek and spin the bottle.

'There is no way I'm doing any of that,' said Zeke. 'I would rather live in a toilet.'

'Me too,' replied the Man in the Moon. 'We've got to jump off here before we're violently ill.'

'Not on your life,' laughed the girls' leader, a tall strong girl with bright red hair called Vanessa Venus. 'There's no way you're running away from us, and I'm going to make sure of it!' And with that she threw a handful of pink-magic-kissing dust at Zeke and Moonie and then began to laugh loudly. 'This will make you want to hug and kiss us every minute of every day for the rest of your lives.'

Well it worked on Moonie, who was so

completely covered by the magic dust that it even went into his ears, nose, eyes and mouth. But it didn't work at all on Zeke because he is allergic to dust and he just sneezed it all off.

'Quick!' yelled Zeke. 'Off we go.'

'No, I'm very happy here,' said Moonie as he kissed and cuddled the gaggle of girls.

So Zeke jumped from the skycycle handlebars with a 'yahoo' and luckily landed on the roof of a passing space taxi, which was a free service provided by the local council and looked a bit like a chocolate doughnut but moved a whole lot faster.

'To Planet Sock, please,' Zeke said to the driver, who was a small slimy yellow fellow with three heads.

'Of course, of course, of course,' the driver replied, and so off they went.

Pretty soon they caught up with

Neptune and Nipper and were close enough to even overhear their secret conversation, which was about Prince Nipper not keeping his bedroom tidy enough, and therefore not being allowed to watch any TV until he'd picked everything up.

Suddenly the Neptunes spotted Zeke and drew their special silver arrows to fire at him as he passed. But the cab driver drove like a football star, ducking and weaving and spinning and turning and never once receiving even a scratch on his bumper bar. The Neptunes were furious. Who was this smarty pants? And they ordered their horses to fly faster.

Leaping over planets and galloping across galaxies, they raced at a pace through space until Zeke arrived on Planet Sock a good ten minutes before the Neptunes.

'Thank you,' Zeke said to the cab

driver as he waved him goodbye.

Thinking he was all alone, Zeke started to wander about Planet Sock and soon realised the entire planet was made out of nothing but socks. The ground was socks, the trees were socks, the cars, the houses, the pets and the people were all socks.

'Aha,' thought Zeke. 'I get it now! Planet Sock's the place where all those socks go when they disappear from the washing.' (Suddenly he remembered home, and the hurry he was in to rescue his sister and get his yo-yo back before his snoring mum woke up.)

'Hello,' said a red sock.

'Hello,' said Zeke. 'I'm wondering if you can help me. Have you seen a silly girl called Eppie who has a yo-yo stuck in her hair?'

'What did you say?' said the red sock. 'A silly girl called Eppie? Officers!

Arrest this boy!'

'Why?' squeaked Zeke. 'What have I
done?'

'You've spoken badly of our queen,
you traitor!'

'What?' said Zeke. 'Stupid Eppie is
your queen?'

'Double arrest this man,' said the red
sock. And with that a whole army of
socks (about a drawer full) arrested Zeke
(but only once, because they didn't have
a clue how to double arrest anything).

Anyway, the socks took Zeke off to
jail, and may I say the socks all
marched very well, and when they got
to the jail it was also made of socks,
boys' sports socks, and they

stank!

But that's where Zeke sat, in the
pongo sock jail for what seemed like

days and days and days, but was probably about fifteen minutes. Then there was a fanfare of trumpets (which actually sounded a little muffled because socks are not great trumpet players) and Zeke was escorted to the magnificent Sock Garden, which quite honestly just looked like a pile of washing.

'All rise to meet Her Majesty,' said the leader of the army, a rather attractive tall blue sock with a gold circle round the top. And with that Queen Eppie arrived.

'Hello, stranger in a cheese suit. My name is Queen Eppie. Welcome to my Queendom.'

'Eppie, it's me,' whispered Zeke.

'Me *who*?' replied Queen Eppie.

'Me, Zeke your brother, you stupid idiot!'

'Aaaaaagh, don't you call me a stupid idiot,' said Eppie, 'or I won't tell you that

I've been lying here really missing home
while I listened to Mum and her
snoring.'

'Missing home!' said Zeke, not
believing. 'What is there to miss? Here
you're a queen and spoilt rotten.'

'Well actually, Zeke, I'm pretty bored.
Whenever I want to get up and do
anything some sock goes and does it for
me.'

'Gosh, Eppie,' scolded Zeke. 'Have you

been hit on the head? You used to be the laziest fuzzhead that I've ever met, and I was quite proud of you. Anyone else would dream of this life. I can only imagine that you're very ill and I must get you home immediately, because other than that you're an ungrateful dingbat.'

'Am not.'

'Are so.'

'Am not.'

'Are too.'

'Guards!' called Eppie. 'Take this silly boy away and hang him from the clothesline.'

And hundreds of socks came towards Zeke, making frightening faces as they marched. But they actually looked cute instead of scary and Zeke wanted to reach down and cuddle them. Luckily, however, he came to his senses and, as the sock guards reached out for Zeke, he grabbed the whole bunch and tied them up in a knot.

'Now come with me,' Zeke ordered his sister.

'No, I've changed my mind,' said Eppie. 'You're absolutely right about this place being good. So I've decided that this is where I should stay.'

'Well, that's bad luck 'cause I'm taking you home.'

'But . . .' said Eppie.

'There's no time for buts,' said Zeke urgently as he heard the distant thunder of hooves. 'I have to take you right here and now because King Neptune is somewhere here on this planet, ready to kidnap you and make you marry his son!'

'Oh fantastic!' said Eppie. 'Then I'm definitely staying. I hear Prince Nipper is gorgeous.'

'You come with me, Eppie,' ordered Zeke. 'Or else I'm snitching to Mum.'

The flying horses were coming closer.

Zeke jumped for cover up a green sock tree and the socks shrieked, screamed and squelched (which is a sort of high piercing noise that socks make when they're afraid).

But Eppie stood very straight right in the middle of the garden, smoothing her hair, neatening her gown, fluttering her eyelids like a film star and trying to make her bosoms look enormous, even though she actually didn't have any.

'I hope he's rich,' wished Eppie. 'With a boat and a palace and a sister I can play with. And I hope I shall have beautiful clothes and jewels and parties and cakes and lollies. And I hope that he is as handsome as a dream.'

The flurry of horses came closer and halted right before Eppie. She waited for the sock dust and lint to settle, then slowly opened her eyes while puckering her lips as though ready for a most romantic kiss . . . and lo and behold if she didn't get a kiss, a great big wet sloppy kiss that smelt a lot like fish.

'Oh gross!' screamed Eppie as she opened her eyes and saw that Prince Nipper was a fishhead.

'Aaaaaaaaaaaaaaaaaaaaa aaaaaaaaaaaaaaaaaaaaaaaa aaaaaaaaaaaaaaaaaaaaaaaa aaaaaaaaaaaaaaaaaaaaaaaa aaaaaaaaaaaaaaaaaaaaaaaa aaaaaaaaaagh!' shrieked Eppie.

'Follow me,' yelled Zeke.

But Nipper had grabbed Queen Eppie with his slimy fish fins and was laughing delightedly.

'Help,' Eppie blurted out. 'Help me, Zeke. I promise I'll eat all your yucky vegetables for absolutely ever.'

Suddenly Eppie thought she needn't have bothered to make such a big promise because Nipper was so slippery he was losing his grip on her anyway, and down she slid, swish boom bah, and landed softly on the sock ground underneath. But she still needed rescuing.

'Do you promise you'll eat my yucky vegetables?' demanded Zeke.

'Yes,' said Eppie sulkily.

'Pinky then,' said Zeke holding out his little finger.

'Pinky,' said Eppie touching Zeke's little finger with hers. And so the deal was done. Eppie would eat Zeke's yucky vegetables and Zeke would rescue her. Then before you could say 'sock a doodle do' the brother and sister were holding hands and running away as fast as they could.

'After them!' yelled King Neptune. And off they went through the sock town, chasing Queen Eppie and Zeke, over the sock bridge, past the sock tower, through the sock shops, the sock schools and the sock hospital that was busy repairing all the sick socks with holes in their heels and their toes.

'Dive,' yelled Zeke.

'Dive where?' yelled Eppie.

'This is no time for questions,' scolded Zeke as he picked Eppie up by the scruff of the neck and threw her into a huge football sock that was on his way home from a game, and then threw himself in straight after.

'Sssssshh,' said Queen Eppie to the football sock. 'Don't tell a sole we're in here.' ("Sole", get it?)

'Of course, Your Majesty. You smell like fish, I assume you're escaping from Prince Nipper? Leave it up to me.'

And they were all perfectly quiet as the football sock walked to the airport with his precious cargo, and no one would ever have known what he was hiding inside if it weren't for one very simple thing – Zeke's yo-yo was still attached to Eppie's head and poking out the top.

'There they are!' yelled King

Neptune. And so the football sock ran
as fast as he could while his passengers
cried, 'Help us!'

But no one paid any attention
because they couldn't quite understand
what Zeke and Eppie had said.

'Melt us? What does that mean?' said
the sock crowd that had gathered.

'No,' yelled Queen Eppie. 'Help us.'

'Oh, eat puss!' said the crowd. 'Well
that really is disgusting.'

'No, you ninnies!' roared Queen

Eppie. 'For heaven's sake, catch those suckers behind us.'

And the sock people replied, 'Oh, OK.' But the socks had absolutely no luck at all. They tried lying on the road and tripping the baddies. They even tried jumping from the trees and strangling the Neptunes. But absolutely nothing seemed to work and the Neptunes were only a few horse lengths away as Zeke and Eppie and the football sock entered Planet Sock Airport.

'When is the next flight to Earth?' said the football sock to the frilly sock airport receptionist.

'Oh we haven't any direct flights to Earth,' she said. 'We only have a falling star that is going to Mercury, and a comet that is going to Jupiter.'

'Have you nothing at all that is going to Earth?' begged Queen Eppie from inside the footy sock.

'Is that you, Queen Eppie?' said the receptionist. 'I'll see what I can do.'

The Neptunes were stopped for a moment by a pair of socks who tried to wrap round their eyes like blind-folds, but soon their war cries could be heard again charging even closer.

The receptionist rang her very hot boyfriend to see what he could do. 'He's a meteor,' explained the frilly sock. 'And although he is supposed to go to the sun to refuel, he said he'll drop you off at Earth on the way.'

'Yeh,' yahooed Zeke and Eppie as a blinding flash and a ball of light landed on the tarmac ready to take them home.

They ran as fast as fast across the tarmac with the Neptunes in frightening pursuit. Closer and closer, they could smell their fishy breath!

'Oh no, this is the end!' cried Zeke and Eppie as King Neptune lowered his enormous fork and prepared to scoop the children up like two peas on a plate.

'Ouch,' said Zeke.

'Ouch,' said Eppie when the prongs of the fork poked and prodded them as King Neptune tried to take perfect aim.

'Aaaaaaaaaaaaagh,' they both squeaked as they were scooped up at last by the horrible Neptunes, who were laughing with glee until . . . suddenly a huge sock-trap dropped from high above the tarmac and captured the Neptunes like fish in a net, leaving only the fork poking outside and its passengers, Zeke and Eppie.

'Phew,' said Zeke and Eppie as they climbed on board the meteor just in time, and waved thank you to the clever socks. Then they swooped and glided through the night.

It was very relaxing and the children were feeling good until they noticed, after a while, that the morning sun was teasing on the horizon and it was about to rise and wake the world.

'Mum will be getting up pretty soon,' whispered Eppie. 'I hope we're back in time!'

'I know,' said Zeke, 'I'm worried too. It feels like we're going far too

s l o w l y wa

AA

AAA

AAH.'

Suddenly faster and faster they went, faster and faster and faster as they entered Earth's atmosphere!

The pressure of the speed stretched and pulled them: their faces, their arms, their legs, their bodies, their ears, their noses, their fingers and toes. Stretch, stretch, pull, pull – on it went all the way back to Earth. Until Zeke and Eppie were finally dropped off at their front door, both as thin as a piece of skinny spaghetti and as tall as a telegraph pole.

'Oh look at *you*,' Eppie laughed, as the light of the sun began to shine and they could finally see each other clearly.

'Well look at *you*,' said Zeke poking his long tongue out. 'And anyway, at least my yo-yo's still safe on your head and that's really all that matters.'

'Is not all that matters.'

'Is so.'

'Is not.'

'Is so.'

'Is not.'

And then they paused because they were both out of breath. And when they stopped fighting they could hear . . . nothing.

Absolutely nothing.
Complete and utter silence.
(shhhhh)

'Oh no!' Zeke and Eppie gasped together. 'Mum's stopped snoring. She must be waking up.' Aaaaaaaaaaaaagh panic panic panic panic.

'All we have to do,' said Zeke at last, when he'd finally calmed himself down, 'is get back to normal size and then Mum will never know the difference. So, first things first, let's go into our house.'

Which they did, by the easiest, quietest way they could, which was sliding underneath the front door.

But when Zeke and Eppie stood up they didn't fit under the ceiling, so they crouched as low as possible, bending over backwards, rolled into balls, and full of fear they tip-toed up the stairs. And they saw their mum was still sort of asleep, only just starting to stir and mumbling and rumbling something about starting a music group with her friends and calling it the Spice Mums.

'Quick, into the bathroom!' said Eppie to Zeke. 'And we'll work out what to do.'

'Well I've already got a plan, you stupid bossy boots,' said Zeke as they closed the bathroom door. 'I think if we run on the spot till we get really hot, we'll go like warm soft plasticine and we can mould ourselves back into shape.'

'Good idea, for once,' said Eppie. 'So come on, let's get started.'

'No, first,' said Zeke, 'just to make sure

this trouble never happens again, I think we should remove the yo-yo from your hair. So let's put shampoo all over your head, to make the hair slippery so the yo-yo will slide off . . . absolutely easy peezy.'

'Good idea number two,' said Eppie throwing her arms into the air with excitement and knocking Mum's perfumes off the cabinet so the bottles went smashing to the ground.

Snort, came the noise from Mum's bedroom. Oh no, she was waking up!

'Quick put the plug in the bath and stick your hair exactly under the tap,' said Zeke as he poured shampoo all over Eppie's head.

They could hear Mum's door opening wide and any minute they'd hear her footsteps coming down the hall.

'Rub your hair, Eppie, to make it all slippery.'

But still the yo-yo wouldn't come out. So desperately, Zeke added more shampoo and more and more and more, and before you know it the bath started to fill, and then began to overflow.

'I've got it!' said Zeke as the room filled with bubbles. 'I've removed the yo-yo from your hair. So turn the tap off and let the plug out immediately.'

But Eppie couldn't see where the plug was because of all the bubbles and the bathroom started to fill with water and enormous fabulous froth.

'What on earth is that coming under the bathroom door?' said Mum as she came stumbling down the hallway.

'Mum's coming!' yelled Zeke.

'Mum's coming!' yelled Eppie.

And they splashed around among the

bubbles, grabbing at this and that and finally Eppie found the plug, pulled at it hard and the water went racing with enormous force, tumbling thankfully down the drain. But unfortunately so did long, skinny Eppie.

'Who's in there?' said Mum as she knocked on the bathroom door.

'Whoever you are, you're in the most humungous trouble and I'm coming in to get you.'

And, with that, spaghetti Zeke dived down the plughole after Eppie.

And Mum, who still hadn't found her glasses, walked straight into the laundry cupboard and got really angry with a broom.

About the author, Gretel Killeen;

Gretel Killeen started writing comedy by accident when she stood up to perform a very serious poem and everybody laughed.

From here she moved to writing and performing comedy in a variety of theatres and clubs across her home country, Australia, and for a number of major radio stations. Gretel's comedy writing then led to television and in 2001 Gretel hosted Australia's *Big Brother* – a phenomenal success which she repeated in 2002.

Gretel has published a number of best-selling books that will split your sides and make your head explode. After you read them, you'll never be the same again.

She lives in Sydney's famous Bondi with her two children, Zeke and Eppie – the stars of *My Sister's a Yo-yo* and *My Sister's an Alien*.